Peaches Pie, Take a Bath!

Based on the episode written by Ed Valentine
Adapted by Bill Scollon
For the series created by Chris Nee
Illustrated by Character Building Studio and the Disney Storybook Art Team

ABDOBOOKS.COM

Reinforced library bound edition published in 2019 by Spotlight, a division of ABDO, PO Box 398166, Minneapolis, Minnesota 55439. Spotlight produces high-quality reinforced library bound editions for schools and libraries. Published by agreement with Disney Press, an imprint of Disney Book Group.

Printed in the United States of America, North Mankato, Minnesota.
092018   012019

DISNEY PRESS
New York • Los Angeles

THIS BOOK CONTAINS
RECYCLED MATERIALS

Library of Congress Control Number: 2017961154

Publisher's Cataloging-in-Publication Data

Names: Scollon, Bill, author. | Valentine, Ed, author. | Character Building Studio; Disney Storybook Art Team, illustrators.
Title: Doc McStuffins: Peaches Pie, take a bath! / by Bill Scollon and Ed Valentine; illustrated by Character Building Studio and Disney Storybook Art Team.
Description: Minneapolis, MN : Spotlight, 2019 | Series: World of reading level pre-1
Summary: When Alma's dog, Rudy, drags Peaches Pie through the mud, the sweet smelling doll suddenly doesn't smell so peachy. Can Doc help her?
Identifiers: ISBN 9781532141782 (lib. bdg.)
Subjects: LCSH: Doc McStuffins (Television program)--Juvenile fiction. | Toys--Juvenile fiction. | Personal cleanliness--Juvenile fiction. | Baths--Juvenile fiction. | Readers (Primary)--Juvenile fiction.
Classification: DDC [E]--dc23

Spotlight
A Division of ABDO
abdobooks.com

It is a rainy day.
Doc is at Emmie's house.

Her name is Peaches Pie.
She smells like peaches!

Rudy the dog runs in.
He is all wet!

Rudy grabs Peaches Pie.
Come back, Rudy!

The girls chase Rudy.

"Let go!" says Alma.

Rudy lets go.

Peaches Pie is all wet.
She smells like wet dog.

Alma is sad.
Doc will help!

11

The Doc is in!
The toys come to life.

"Something smells like wet dog," says Peaches Pie.

The King wants a checkup.
Doc will see him first.

Lambie starts her dance class.
Peaches is a good dancer.

Hermie dances close to Peaches.

Her dress is smelly.

Doc is ready for Peaches.
"Time for your checkup!" she says.

Chilly whispers to Doc.
"Her dress smells bad."

"You have Soggy-Dog-atosis," says Doc.

Peaches is sad.

Doc knows what to do.

Peaches Pie needs a bath!

Everyone helps Peaches get clean.

"You're all sweet as pie!"
Peaches says.

Peaches Pie is peachy clean!

Oh! Emmie and Alma are coming.
The toys go stuffed.

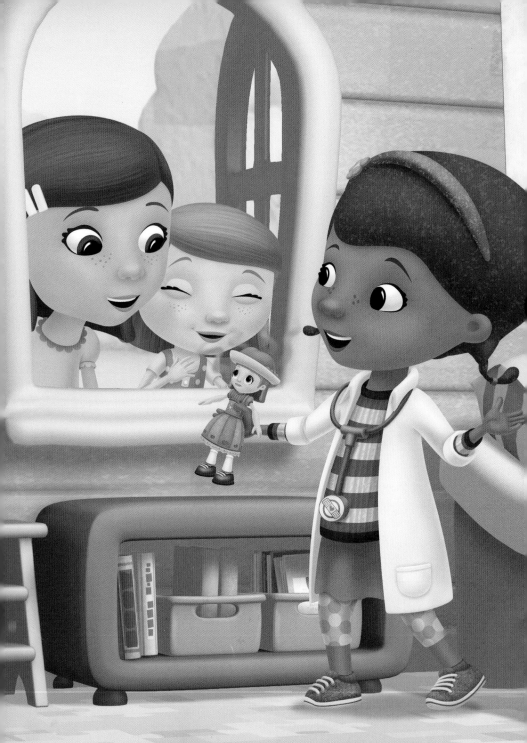

Peaches Pie smells like peaches again!

Peaches feels better.
She is ready to go home.

Thanks, Doc!